Snowzilla

By **Janet Lawler**

Illustrated by **Amanda Haley**

Amazon Children's Publishing

Amazon Publishing
Attn: Amazon Children's Books
P.O. Box 400818
Las Vegas, NV 89149
www.amazon.com/amazonchildrenspublishing

Library of Congress Cataloging-in-Publication Data
Lawler, Janet.
Snowzilla / by Janet Lawler ;
illustrated by Amanda Haley. — 1st ed.
p. cm.
Summary: When neighbors complain that her snowman is too tall, Cami
Lou finds a perfect new place for him in the community garden.
ISBN 978-0-7614-6188-3 (hardcover)
ISBN 978-0-7614-6190-6 (ebook)
[1. Stories in rhyme. 2. Snowmen—Fiction.]
I. Haley, Amanda, ill. II. Title.
PZ8.3.L355Sno 2012   [E]—dc23   2011036611

The illustrations are rendered in acrylics
and colored pencil.

Book design by Vera Soki
Editor: Marilyn Brigham

Printed in China (W)
First edition
10 9 8 7 6 5 4 3 2 1

To my writers' group—
a talented troupe
—J. L.

To happy snowman builders everywhere
—A. H.

It snowed without stopping
for week after week.
When it ended at last,
Cami Lou took a peek.

She bundled and booted
and zipped up her brother.
"Let's build a huge snowman
unlike any other!"

They packed a large snowball
and pushed it around.
Then Mom plowed the yard,
dumping snow in a mound.

They rolled out a middle
as plump as a pig;
placed a head on the top
with the help of Dad's rig.

They scavenged for buttons,
a hat, and big eyes,
for a nose, and a mouth,
and for arms the right size.

Then Cami Lou cheered
as she stood down below.
"We'll call you Snowzilla!
Our giant of snow!"

Thousands of people rode buses to see
the towering snowman, as tall as a tree.

But neighbors complained and a few acted wild.
They organized quickly and lawsuits were filed.

NO snowzilla!

melt the Snow-man!

No snow-man

SNOWMAN, NO MAN!

"Poochie is scared to go out the front door."

Another said, "Views were much better before."

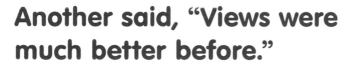

A lady warned everyone, "Make no mistake— when temperatures rise, he'll turn into a lake!"

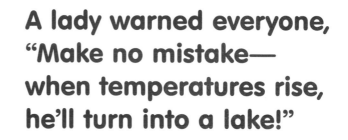

A judge ruled, "Snowzilla will have to come down.
He's too big a threat to the peace in our town."

So Cami used e-mail and texting and blogging
to save all their effort spent packing and slogging.

She contacted cousins and friends that she knew.
"Snowzilla's in danger. Help! What can we do?"

At dawn the next day
a man backed up his truck
and measured Snowzilla.
"I think we're in luck!"

People brought lumber
and scaffolding, too;
hot chocolate and muffins
as snacks for the crew.

Then Cami, her brother,
and other kind folks
all labored together
and told snowman jokes.

They hoisted Snowzilla
up just a few inches
by using a forklift,
and pulleys, and winches.

Parading down Main Street,
they stopped near the square.
Cami Lou pointed.
"Please, set him down there!"

The community garden
was wide open space.
He'd belong to them all
in this perfect new place.

Snowzilla was patted
by dozens of hands,
while everyone sang
to the town's marching bands.

Weeks later, the sun
became hotter and bright.
Snowzilla grew smaller
and flowed out of sight.

Cami Lou waved,
hardly shedding a tear . . .

. . . because she had *much* bigger plans for next year.